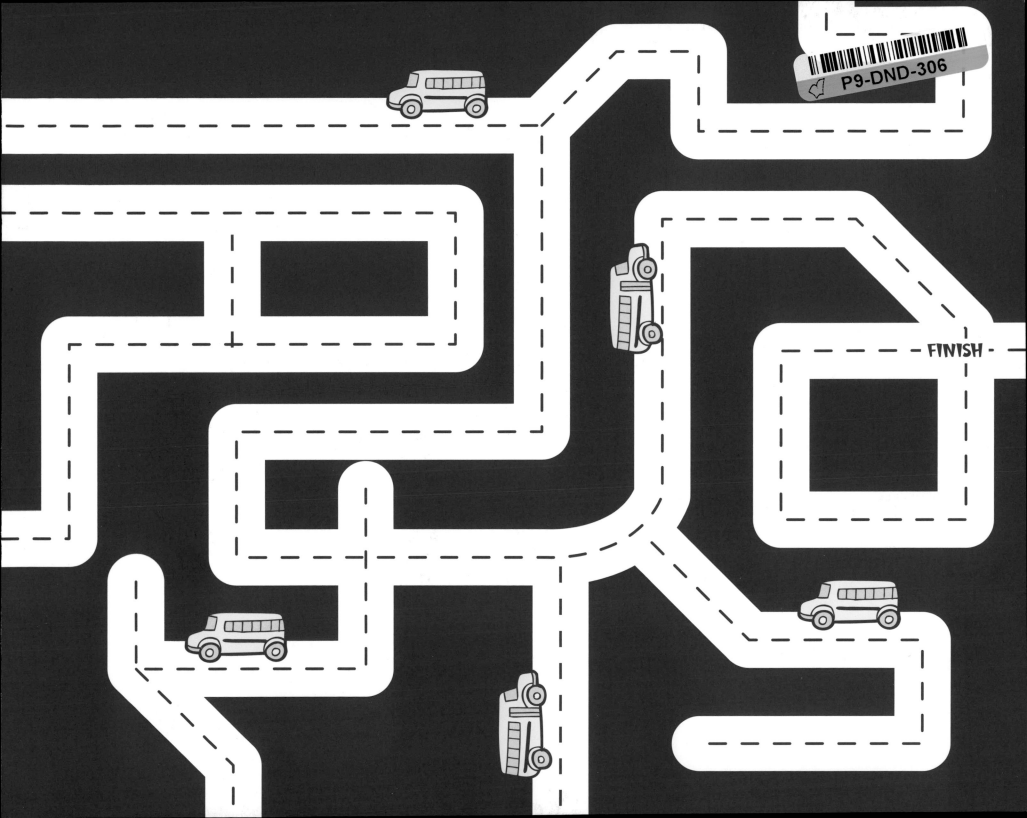

MUMBO JUMBO

Mabel's World

Library of Congress Control Number: 2009934033
Cataloging-in-Publication Data

D'Amico, Christine.
    Mumbo jumbo / by Christine D'Amico ; illustrated by Darcy Bell-Myers.
    p. cm. — (Mabel's world ; 2)
    SUMMARY: On a library field trip, Mabel and Max learn
    how and why new words are added to the dictionary. When
    they get lost, they find many opportunities to use their
    own new word, "mumbo jumbo."
    Audience: Ages 3-10
    ISBN-13: 978-0-9716631-2-1
    ISBN-10: 0-9716631-2-2

    1. English language—Dictionaries—Juvenile fiction.
    2. Encyclopedias and dictionaries—Juvenile fiction.
    3. Lexicology—Juvenile fiction. [1. English language—
    Dictionaries—Fiction. 2. Encyclopedias and
    dictionaries—Fiction. 3. English language—
    Dictionaries. 4. Encyclopedias and dictionaries.]
    I. Bell-Myers, Darcy, ill. II. Title. III. Series.

    PZ7.D18375Mum 2010   [E]
                                    QBI09-600189

10 9 8 7 6 5 4 3 2 1
Printed and bound in Canada by Friesens, Altona, Manitoba

The design is by Darcy Bell-Myers at www.bellmyers.com

MUMBO JUMBO

Mabel's World

Written by Christine D'Amico
Illustrated by Darcy Bell-Myers

ATTITUDE press, Inc.

To Billy and Grandpa Steve, two people dedicated to helping others learn new words.
We Miss You — C.D.

To my darling Amelia — beautiful ballerina, princess and budding reader!
Love always, Mama.

Finally, it was **field trip day**— the first field trip of the year— and Mabel had been looking forward to it all week. She poured cereal into her bowl and sped her finger through the maze on the back of the box. Her older sister Annabelle came down and put her bowl on the table next to Mabel.

MILK MILK

"What a lot of mumbo jumbo," Mabel said to herself.

"What did you say?" asked Annabelle.

"**Mumbo jumbo**. The rules for this maze contest are complete **mumbo jumbo**."

Annabelle cracked a small smile. "Mumbo jumbo," she repeated. "Let me guess—it's another one of your new words from school."

"Sure is," Mabel said. "And isn't it fun to say?"

"I don't know," Annabelle said with a shrug.

"Well, say it a few times and see what you think."

"**Mumbo jumbo**, **MUMBO JUMBO**, MUUMMBBOO JUUMMBBOO. It is kind of fun," Annabelle said, taking another bite of cereal.

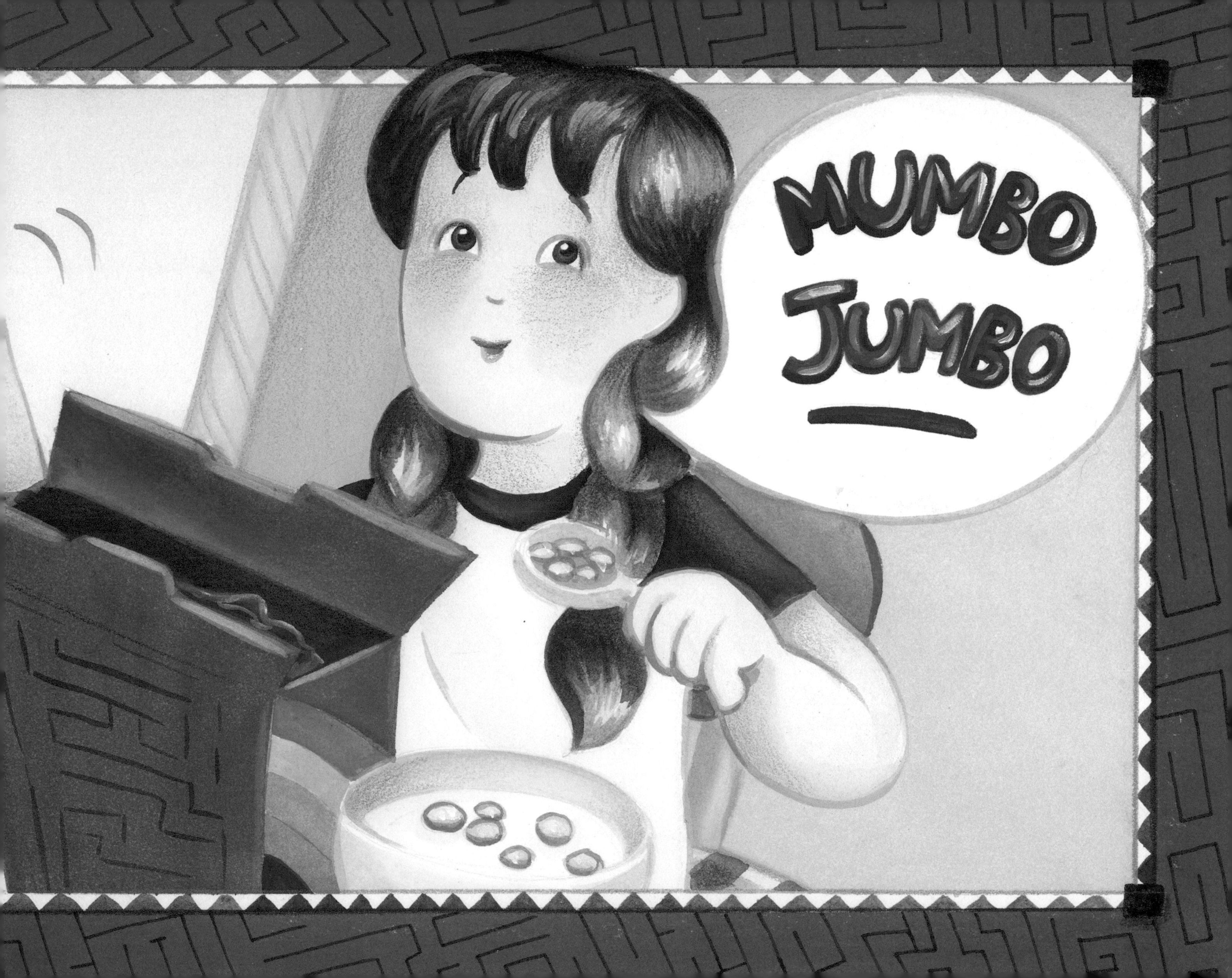
MUMBO JUMBO ___

"You ready for your **big adventure?**" Mom asked as she came into the kitchen juggling a higgledy-piggledy stack of papers along with Mabel's backpack. "It's time to leave, so finish up."

"Just a few more bites of cereal Mom, and I'll be ready," answered Mabel, as she sloshed some milk into her bowl and gobbled up her breakfast.

In no time at all, Mabel was boarding the bus for the field trip.

"A field trip to the library is going to be **boring**," complained Mabel's friend Max. "I wish we were going to the zoo like everyone else."

"It could be fun," said Mabel. "I love going downtown, and my mom said it's a brand new building."

"I was just at this library with my dad," said Max, "and it wasn't even close to fun. I had to be really quiet, and everyone spoke in **mumbo jumbo** that made no sense to me."

Mabel smiled, "Isn't that a fun word to say? I'm so glad Vanessa picked it out of our word bag yesterday!"

"Yeah," said Max. "It's my favorite word right now!"

"Hey, maybe we'll find a new word at the library that we like even better than mumbo jumbo," Mabel said.

"Maybe," Max said with a shrug. "And maybe we'll see a real live **dinosaur**, but I don't think so."

With that they were at the library and heading up the front steps.

"Welcome children," said Ms. Walderword, the librarian. "Today, we are going to give you a tour of our new library." She ushered the children into a large room with walls covered in newspapers. "We'll begin over here."

"This is the newspaper room," said Ms. Walderword. "Every day, we get newspapers delivered from around the world. This one, for example, is from China. And over here is our financial paper; it is one of our most popular papers."

Mabel and Max took a closer look at both papers as they walked by. "Complete **mumbo jumbo**," Mabel said, wrinkling her nose.

"Definitely," Max said.

Ms. Walderword led the children into another room and over to a very large book. "This is the largest book in our collection," she said proudly. "It's a **dictionary**."

"That is the biggest book I've ever seen," Vanessa said, holding her arms out to match the length of the open book.

"It is the biggest book we have," the librarian said, smiling at the girl's exaggerated expression. "This book tells us the definition of almost all of the words in our English language. It helps us learn how to pronounce each word, and it even tells you something about the origins of the word, which means its history and where it came from."

"So this must be where you go to find out if a word is **real**," said Max.

"Well, this is where I go to check out the meaning of a word I don't know or to confirm the spelling of a word, but being in the dictionary is not what makes a word real," said the librarian. The kids looked up at her with puzzled faces. "Words become real when they're used a lot and become a part of our common language. When this happens, the word is then added to the dictionary."

Mabel's eyes widened, "So you mean if we made up a word and then enough people started to use it, our new word would be added to the dictionary?"

"Well, yes. I suppose that could happen," answered the librarian.

"Let's do it!" shouted Vanessa.

"**Yes! Let's do it!**" cheered the children all together.

"How about a new word for good-bye?" Max suggested to Mabel. All of the children were now speaking at once, making up their own new words. The noise caught the attention of everyone around them.

"It's a great idea, but we have to do it quietly," whispered the librarian trying to hush the excited children. "Why don't you continue to think about your new words as we move on to our next room." And she hurried the noisy class out of the dictionary room and into the hallway.

Mabel and Max followed along at the back of the group. However, they were so deep in conversation about the possibilities of a new word for good-bye that they didn't notice when the class made a quick turn to the left.

Instead, the two of them kept walking straight and ended up in a large and crowded room.

Mabel and Max looked around for their classmates, but the room was so full of big kids, it was hard to see very far.

"**What should we do?**" Max asked nervously.

"I don't know," said Mabel. "I don't see our class anywhere."

"Let's just wait here," Max suggested. "We'll find them when these bigger kids leave."

"Good idea," Mabel said as she and Max took seats in the back and began listening to the speaking professor.

"So, in **review**, photosynthesis is the amazing process by which plants and some bacteria use the energy created by sunlight to produce **GLUCOSE**, a form of sugar. And, **blah, blah, blah**…" The professor just kept going on and on.

Finally, when Max and Mabel didn't know if they could take a minute more, the professor stepped off the stage and headed toward them saying, "Now each of you go out into the library and locate some additional information on photosynthesis."

Instantly, all the big kids left the room.
Mabel and Max stood alone by the door.

The professor walked over. "Do you two have a question about **photosynthesis?**"

"I don't even know what **photo-whatchamacallit** is," answered Mabel. "All I can say is that it seems like a lot of **mumbo jumbo** to me."

"It was **mumbo jumbo** to me too," said Max, nodding nervously. "And besides that," he added quickly, "we can't find our class."

"Are you kids in the right place?" the professor asked, looking more closely at the two children.
"Now that I think about it, you both look a little small to be in the 7th grade."

But words are very powerful, and with them you can make all kinds of things happen, even get yourself found; which is exactly what happened for Mabel and Max. Just as the "**t**" in lost left their lips, Ms. Malou appeared, almost as if by magic, stepping briskly into the room and straightening her coat. "Here you are!" she said, holding out an arm to each child. "I've been looking all over for the two of you."

"We didn't know where you had gone," said a relieved Max.

"You two were so busy with your new word **mumbo jumbo** that you didn't see us take a sharp left back at the beginning of the hall," Ms. Malou said, giving her stern-teacher look. "I hope you have both learned that no matter how excited you may be, you must always pay attention to where you are going whenever you are in a library! You just never know what awaits once inside these doors."

Max and Mabel gave a relieved nod. "Good," Ms. Malou said with a final look at each. "Now it is time to get on the bus and go back to school." And after a deep breath and a smile, she finished with her usual, "*All's well that ends well.*"

The professor put out his hand. "Good-bye young library patrons," he said. Mabel and Max politely took turns giving him a firm handshake.

Then Mabel leaned over and whispered to Max, "Let's use our new word to say good-bye." Max nodded and they burst out together,

"PISH-PASH-DASH!".

Pish-Pash-dash

"What was that?" the professor inquired.

"PISH-PASH-DASH," repeated Max with a mischievous glint in his eye.

"Now that is mumbo jumbo," replied the professor, smiling back at the children.

"It may be **mumbo jumbo** now," said Max.

"But just wait," Mabel jumped in, "everyone is going to start saying it, and in a few weeks you'll probably find it added to the dictionary."

"**What?!**" the scientist asked, giving a startled look at Ms. Malou.

She smiled and gave a knowing nod saying, "Stranger things have happened."

Then Ms. Malou took each child by the hand, and they turned to join the rest of the class on the waiting school bus.

Mumbo Jumbo

1. Speech or writing that is unnecessarily obscure.
2. Complicated activities or language that obscures and confuses.

Use the Word in Your Own Life

1. From which friends do you hear the most mumbo jumbo?
2. What was your most recent mumbo jumbo moment?
3. What mumbo jumbo makes you laugh the hardest?
4. What mumbo jumbo do you notice your parents or grandparents are really interested in?
5. What do you do when something you're learning at school begins to seem like hard-to-understand mumbo jumbo?

Activities

1. Make up a word of your own, and create a formal definition of it as you would find in the dictionary. Use your word at school or at home and see if other people start using it too.

2. Go to your library and look at the biggest dictionary that they have. (Maybe their largest dictionary is actually accessed on the computer!) Look up the word "mumbo jumbo" in this large dictionary.

3. Partner up with your parents and go onto the Internet to see what you can learn about fun new words. Some great searches to try are "new English words," "made-up words dictionary," "dictionaries," and "biggest dictionary in the world." There are all kinds of great sites about words with these fun search phrases.

4. Make up your own Mumbo Jumbo Maze. See if you can build new words into your maze in some fun and creative ways.

5. Learn another fun-to-say new word by checking out the book **Higgledy-Piggledy**, the first in the *Mabel's World* series.

6. Most of all, have fun learning new words! There are some really cool ones out there.

START

and one very sleepy child.

SQUiRREL, KoaLa, TiGER, WOLF...

I sigh and pull back the blanket.
"Come on," I say, and in crawl
OWL, BEAR, SNAKE, KITTY, FAWN,

Silence falls over the house. Half asleep,
Dad and I slip into our bed.
We hear one small toddler whisper,

You LOPE back to bed
before Bear can miss you.
"Bathroom,"
you say
out loud

and
hop up